The Tale of Josephine Rose:
A Horse's Magical Neigh

by Kristen Halverson

Illustrated by Kathy Jurek

Francesca,
Enjoy this special
book. :)
Kristen Halverson
2016

First published by Dog Ear Publishing
4011 Vincennes Rd
Indianapolis, IN 46268
www.dogearpublishing.net

ISBN: 978-1-4575-4383-8

This book is printed on acid-free paper.

Printed in the United States of America

Dedication:

To Tempo, my treasured equine companion,
who showed me how to stand tall through challenges and demonstrate grace.

A portion of all book proceeds will benefit the
University of Kentucky Gluck Equine Research Center.

Once upon a time, there was a noble Clydesdale horse named Josephine Rose. She was born on a farm in Canada and spent her life pulling a fancy carriage at local fairs. Josephine Rose stood as tall as a gigantic knight in shining armor. She had feathery hair on her legs that sparkled in the snow and sunlight. Josephine Rose had a red fur coat, a gray, bushy flowing mane, and long eyelashes. But her most special quality was her heart of gold. She was always kind to everyone she met. Josephine Rose retired from pulling carriages and moved to a new farm in the rolling hills of Iowa. There she met a new group of horse friends.

Spaha was an enchanting racehorse from Kentucky. Spaha loved to run fast and spent her early years competing against other horses. She enjoyed jumping across the sparkling creeks on the farm and eating yummy carrots. Spaha was the sweetest horse in the land and was the kind of friend everyone wished they had. She was a great listener, thoughtful, and always understanding to her horse friends on the farm. Spaha had a shiny, dark brown coat, a tiny white dot on her forehead, and a pretty black flowing mane and tail.

Willhanna was the oldest horse on the farm. He, too, was a racehorse, who competed against other horses in Texas when he was younger. Willhanna was very intelligent, powerful, and athletic. He had a bright, orange-chestnut coat, and crooked stripe down his face.

Willhanna loved to run up and down the farm's large, heavenly hill. He also liked to swim in the pond and enjoyed eating carrot spice cookies each evening. He did not like to share his food, though, with any of his horse friends and would grumble and kick when it was feeding time. Willhanna often shared his wisdom with the other horses. They all enjoyed listening to his stories. He loved talking about his racing days and his coaches. They inspired him to never give up and always try his best.

Valentine was the next oldest horse in the herd. She had a tan coat with a wavy brown mane. Valentine lived on a Texas ranch when she was younger and enjoyed working with cattle. She was very playful and loved to throw her food bowl up in the air.

She liked to crunch fresh apples right from the trees. Valentine spent time playing in the sparkling creeks and running with Spaha and Willhanna in the peaceful meadows covered with yellow wildflowers. Valentine was a very tiny horse, but she was proud and brave. She knew she was special even though some of the other horses were bigger and taller.

Josephine Rose was eager to make friends at her new home. The other horses were afraid of her, though, because she looked so different. She was very large because she was a Clydesdale and Josephine Rose spoke a different language than the other horses.

She wanted to be a part of the group, but the other horses ignored her, pushed her out of the barn, and would not let her play with them. Willhanna and Valentine made it clear that they were not interested in being friends.

Spaha wanted to be friends with Josephine Rose, but she felt loyal to Valentine and Willhanna. Because they were older, they seemed to have a great influence on her. Still, Spaha was curious to learn about Josephine Rose and how she was different. Spaha knew in her heart that she needed the courage to speak up to her friends.

She knew her friends didn't like being treated poorly. Willhanna and Valentine had also moved to a new farm with several horses many years ago. They had shared their own stories about how the other horses had ignored them and made them feel unwelcome. Spaha was sad that they treated Josephine Rose badly. After all, they had all been outsiders at one time or another.

Willhanna and Valentine often chased Josephine Rose away. Valentine and Willhanna stood on their back hooves and told Josephine Rose she was not welcome on the farm. They said she could not graze beneath the bright green majestic oak trees on top of the hill, and she couldn't eat with them in the barn.

Spaha tried to talk with her friends about their attitudes and poor choices as the days passed. Willhanna and Valentine replied that they simply did want to learn about Josephine Rose's differences and were happy with their three-horse group. Sharing the barn and pasture with a gigantic horse from a faraway place was uncomfortable to them. They were not interested in making Josephine Rose a friend.

Josephine Rose was very sad and spent the days grazing by herself. The other horses watched her from a distance and were happy she was far away. They giggled and glared at Josephine Rose if she came close to them on the hill. They did not want her to be a part of the group. They laughed and said she was the size of an elephant.

One day, the sun was shining, and the sky was full of friendly clouds. Spaha felt
sad for Josephine Rose because she was all alone. She finally gathered enough
courage to show her friends that being kind to others is very important. She
allowed Josephine Rose to share her grain and hay. Spaha knew the importance
of sharing, because she had moved to a new farm several times. She knew what it
felt like to be an outsider.

Still, Valentine and Willhanna were very grumpy about making friends with a new horse. They continued to eat and play alone together in the rolling green meadows and sparkling creeks. They missed Spaha grazing and playing with them on the heavenly hill and could not understand why she was trying so hard to make Josephine Rose feel welcome. They had never been friends with a Clydesdale horse. She was so different from each of them!

The next day a huge thunderstorm rolled in over the hills, and Josephine Rose was very scared. The sky was dark and full of angry clouds. Even though Spaha had made friends with Josephine Rose, Willhanna and Valentine would not allow Josephine Rose in the barn. The thunder grew louder and louder with each passing moment. It sounded like large barrels were being rolled down from the sky! Josephine Rose was very frightened and shook with fear. She felt all alone and got soaked while standing in the rain.

Spaha saw the fear in Josephine Rose as she stood outside the barn in the storm. Spaha also saw that the storm was becoming worse, and she was worried about her friend's safety. Spaha began to think, How she could be brave? Where was the courage she needed to change her friends' hearts about Josephine Rose?

Just then, a very loud and powerful clap of thunder shook the ground and the entire barn. It gave Spaha courage. She reared up on her hind legs and let out a loud, magical neigh.

"Let her inside the barn, so she is safe with us! She is one of us! We need to make her feel welcome here!" Willhanna and Valentine were surprised by Spaha's bravery and stood in awe of the magical neigh.

As Spaha spoke, the magical neigh created a beautiful and colorful rainbow in the sky. The rainbow made Valentine and Willhanna feel compassion and empathy. Its positive beauty changed their hearts immediately. Surrounded by the magical neigh, they suddenly saw the importance of acceptance, sharing, thoughtfulness, and the true meaning of friendship. They recognized that they were all one herd and needed to respect Josephine Rose's differences.

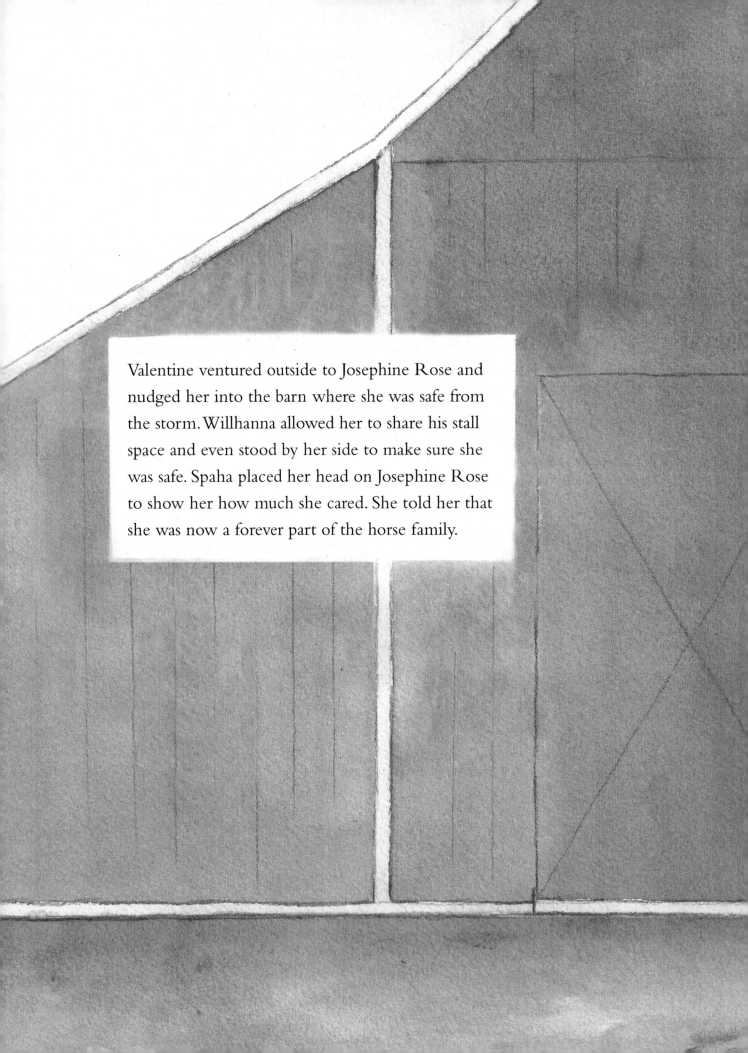

Valentine ventured outside to Josephine Rose and nudged her into the barn where she was safe from the storm. Willhanna allowed her to share his stall space and even stood by her side to make sure she was safe. Spaha placed her head on Josephine Rose to show her how much she cared. She told her that she was now a forever part of the horse family.

As the bright sun shined the next day, all the horses played and grazed on the heavenly hill together. Even though Josephine Rose was from a faraway place and was different because of her size, the other horses learned to love her for her own special qualities. They all galloped into the wind and up the hill together celebrating their new friendship.

The End

CPSIA information can be obtained
at www.ICGtesting.com
Printed in the USA
LVOW05s0053140716

496053LV00017B/61/P

9 781457 543838